MEG AND DAD DISCOVER
Treasure in the Air

LISA WESTBERG PETERS

Illustrations by
DEBORAH DURLAND DeSAIX

Henry Holt and Company · New York

Henry Holt and Company, Inc.
Publishers since 1866
115 West 18th Street
New York, New York 10011

Henry Holt is a registered trademark of Henry Holt and Company, Inc.

Published in Canada by Fitzhenry & Whiteside Ltd.,
195 Allstate Parkway, Markham, Ontario L3R 4T8.

Library of Congress Cataloging-in-Publication Data
Peters, Lisa Westberg.
Meg and dad discover treasure in the air / Lisa Westberg Peters;
illustrations by Deborah Durland DeSaix.
Summary: While walking in the woods, Meg and her dad find some
ancient rocks that were important in creating the oxygen that
supports life on our planet.
[1. Rocks—Fiction.   2. Evolution—Fiction.   3. Fossils—Fiction.
4. Fathers and daughters—Fiction.]   I. DeSaix, Deborah Durland, ill.   II. Title.
PZ7.P44174Me   1995   [Fic]—dc20   95-2039

ISBN 0-8050-2418-2
First Edition—1995

Printed in the United States of America on acid-free paper. ∞

1   3   5   7   9   10   8   6   4   2

The artist used a combination of
watercolor ink and colored pencil
on Canson charcoal paper to create
the illustrations for this book.

For Maxine

—L. W. P.

For George

—D. D. D.

Early in the summer, Meg and her dad took a walk in the woods. The air smelled fresh, scrubbed clean by the rain.

Meg looked for rubies and sapphires, but instead she found rocks that looked like stacks of lumpy pancakes.

Meg bumped them a little with her boots. She didn't see any rubies in them. "They're just plain old rocks," she said.

But her dad stooped down to get a closer look. He ran his fingers along their wavy lines. "Old," he said, "but not plain. You can't imagine what these are."

Meg squeezed her eyes shut and said, "Yes I can."

"Okay," said her dad. "Imagine this. Where you're sitting is not a forest. It's a warm tropical seashore."

"Mmm . . ." said Meg. She liked that idea.

"And it's a long, long time ago," said her dad. "It's about two billion years ago—that's two thousand million years—and the continents are much smaller. There's no life on them at all—no people, no dinosaurs, not even any trees or flowers. The only life is in the sea."

Meg frowned a little. It was hard to imagine land without plants or animals.

"And besides that," said her dad, "there's hardly any oxygen in the air. Since we need oxygen to breathe, this air would be poisonous if we were really there—"

"But we're only imagining," said Meg, holding her breath just the same.

"In the shallow water are big rocky domes with flat tops," said her dad. "They look like giant burnt marshmallows."

"Yum," said Meg. "They're best when they're burnt."

"But you wouldn't like to eat these," said her dad. "The domes are homes for living in."

"I wouldn't want to live in one," said Meg.

"Nope," said her dad. "And you wouldn't fit. But millions of tiny green cells live in a layer on top of the domes. They're not quite plants or animals—something in between."

"Weird," said Meg.

"A little," said her dad.

"All day," he went on, "they use the energy of the sun and two ingredients—water and carbon dioxide—to make food for themselves, just like plants do today. Then they give off bubbles of oxygen."

"They burp?" said Meg, and she giggled.

"Later, when the sun goes down," said her dad, "the cells stop making food. Sand washes in with the waves and currents, and settles on the layer of cells. It stays because the cells are sticky."

"Slimy?" Meg asked.

"Maybe a little slimy," said her dad.

"By morning, the cells have glued the sand to the top of the dome with something like cement. But some of the cells perk up again. They grow up and over the sand to get back into the sunshine. It's like building another room on the roof of your house whenever your room gets too dirty."

"I'd like that," said Meg.

"I bet you would," said her dad.

"Now, do you know what these are?" he asked, tapping the rocks with his boot.

Meg traced the wavy lines, layer upon layer, like squished pancakes.

"These are the little air makers," she declared.

"Almost," said her dad. "These are the fossils of the domes they lived in."

Meg got down close and yelled, "Are you in there?"

Her dad laughed. "They're long gone."

"Did they go extinct like the dinosaurs?" Meg asked.

"Not quite. I'll tell you what happened."

"For millions of years, the air makers built domes on seashores all over Earth, and that's about the only life there was."

"That's it?" Meg gasped.

"That's it," said her dad. "But on those domes were millions of green cells bubbling up oxygen every day for millions of years. That's a lot of oxygen!"

Meg's eyes opened wide at the thought. "But was it enough?" she asked. "Enough air for animals to breathe?" Somehow this seemed to be the most important thing.

"Well, it took a long time," said her dad, "but about a billion years ago, the air makers finally pumped out enough oxygen for animals to be able to live."

"Hurray!" said Meg.

"But," he added, "when sea animals evolved, they were hungry. Some of them, especially snails, found the air makers pretty tasty and munched them nearly to extinction. Today they have to live where there aren't any snails."

"Where's that?" Meg wanted to know. She knew it wasn't her backyard. There were plenty of snails there.

"One of the places is called Shark Bay, on the coast of
Australia."

"Does it have sharks?" Meg asked.

"I don't know," said her dad. "But I do know that it's very salty and most animals don't like it much. So the air makers have it all to themselves—except for a few scientists who go there to learn about life in the past."

"I wish they could live in my yard," said Meg.

Her dad smiled. "You've got a yard full of air makers."

"Oh yeah," Meg said. She forgot. Her yard, her neighborhood, the whole Earth, was now full of plants. Every day they made oxygen. And every day, Meg breathed it.

"But I like the first air makers," she said.

"I do too," said her dad. "Those little green cells were just about the first life on Earth, and they changed the world forever."

"Wow," said Meg, trying to breathe
in the whole idea. She didn't even
have to close her eyes and imagine.
The new world was all around her—
butterflies fluttering, chipmunks
chattering. She would look for rubies
another day. Today the treasure
was in the air.

AUTHOR'S NOTE

The world's oldest fossils are odd-looking lumps called stromatolites (stro-MAT-o-lites). I first saw stromatolites at the top of the Medicine Bow Mountains in Wyoming. The word *stromatolite* means "stony carpet" in Greek, but I thought the fossils looked a lot like cow pies made out of rock. The ones I saw were a billion years old, which was hard for me to imagine, but some stromatolites are even older—3,800 million years old, almost as old as Earth itself. Stromatolites can be found all over the world.

At first their antiquity was all that interested me. But that wasn't the whole story. Cyanobacteria (sy-AN-o-bac-TER-i-a), the tiny organisms that built the domes, pioneered the use of photosynthesis and transformed our atmosphere. Despite their microscopic size, they were huge players in the history of life.

Scientists call the tiny cells cyanobacteria because *cyan* in Greek refers to a color between blue and green, and because the organisms act like bacteria. People used to call them blue-green algae.

Descendants of the earliest cyanobacteria are still around today, but only a few are the dome-making type. Look for slippery green colonies of them on shorelines or in pond water. They are still pumping out oxygen, as they have for eons, but today plants on land and algae in the sea make most of the oxygen we breathe.